WELCOME TO
CAMP CATASTROPHE

by Dick Chodkowski

PRICE STERN SLOAN

Los Angeles

For Flanzy

Library of Congress Cataloging-in-Publication Data
Chodkowski, Dick, 1942—
  Camp Catastrophe / by Dick Chodkowski.
       p.   cm.
  Summary: The misadventures of a group of cat kids at summer camp.
  ISBN 0-8431-2435-0
  [1. Cats—Fiction. 2. Camps—Fiction. 3.Humorous stories.]
I. Title.
PZ7.c44625Cam   1990
[Fic]—dc20
                                                        89-37012
                                                              CIP
                                                               AC

Popsicle® is a registered trademark of
Popsicle Industries, Inc.

Ping-Pong® is a registered trademark of
Harvard Sports Inc.

Copyright © 1989 by Dick Chodkowski
Published in the United States of America by Price Stern Sloan, Inc.
360 North La Cienega Boulevard, Los Angeles, California 90048

ISBN: 0-8431-2435-0

The bus jerked to a stop and everybody began cheering and shouting—everybody except Willard. He couldn't understand why all these kids were so excited about some dumb summer camp.

In fact, he had a feeling this whole week at Camp Catastrophe was going to be a real bummer.

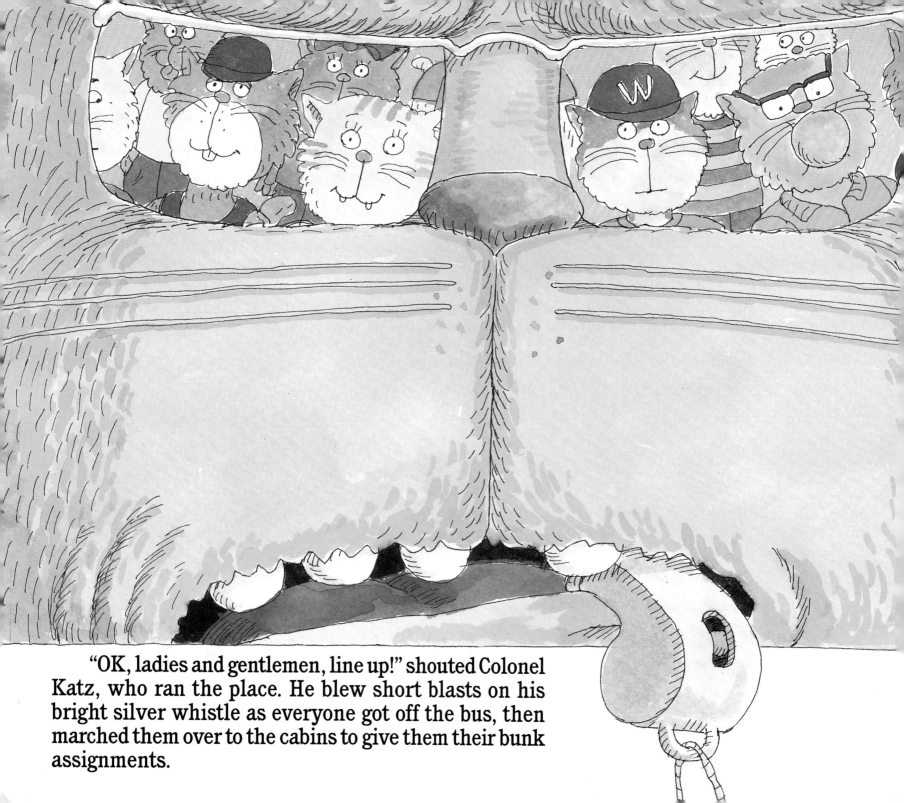

"OK, ladies and gentlemen, line up!" shouted Colonel Katz, who ran the place. He blew short blasts on his bright silver whistle as everyone got off the bus, then marched them over to the cabins to give them their bunk assignments.

Willard ended up sharing his with a younger cat named Buford who was acting goofy. That night, Buford counted backwards from 2,693 to put himself to sleep. It took him three times.

Breakfast the next morning was yucky. There wasn't a bowl of sugary cereal or a bottle of maple syrup within miles of Camp Catastrophe, just tasteless oatmeal and some toast that was supposed to be good for you. Willard could have sworn it was made from tree bark.

That afternoon, Katz took everyone for a canoe ride on the lake. "Stay away from Camp Runamuck," he said, pointing across the water. "Those boys are a nasty bunch!"

Everybody stood up to get a better look—and that's the worst thing a canoeful of cats could have done.

After swimming to shore and pulling in the canoe, the boys and girls dried themselves in the sun. Willard thought about all the TV cartoons he was missing.

The good news that afternoon was that Willard won the blueberry picking contest.

The bad news was that he got a poison ivy rash doing it.

Then during arts and crafts class, Willard sat on a doll house made from Popsicle sticks that looked amazingly like a chair—at least to him.

Willard never realized just how temperamental artists could be, or how fast they could run.

That evening's marshmallow roast was cancelled due to a sudden shortage of marshmallows, so Katz sent everyone back to their cabins to write letters home saying what a great time they were having.

Buford copied Willard's letter exactly.

Well, almost.

The next morning, a messenger came with a special delivery package for the camp. "Hmm...that's funny," said Katz, opening the box. I don't remember ordering any jelly donuts."

"Uh, oh!" he cried, as the contents of the box jumped out and scattered. "Skunks!"

"Run for it, troops!" Katz screamed. "The boys from Camp Runamuck have struck again!"

Since they had been run out of their cabins, Katz decided it was time for an overnight camping trip to lift everyone's spirits.

They all strapped on back packs and off they marched.

Just before sunset Katz admitted they were lost, so he decided they would pitch their tents right where they were—wherever that was.

Naturally, that's when it started raining. Katz acted as center pole while everyone studied the directions. Finally, the tent was up and they all fell asleep, exhausted.

That's when the boys from Camp Runamuck showed up.

Quietly, they glued each sleeping bag shut, then snuck away.

As he hopped back to camp the next morning, Willard decided he'd had enough of Camp Catastrophe.

After lunch Katz assembled everyone for the Ping-Pong tournament. Quietly, Willard slipped away into the woods. "I'll be home before dark, munching marshmallows and watching TV," he thought.

He remembered that the bus ran down by the main highway, which was just on the other side of the woods, which was down the path toward the old fence post. Anyway, you couldn't miss it.

Willard walked for a long time. The woods kept getting thicker with bushes and trees, and nothing looked familiar.

Willard sat down to collect his thoughts. He was tired and hungry. It would be just about supper time back at camp. What he'd give for a bowl of lima beans, or even creamed spinach.

It was getting dark. Willard wondered what kind of wild creatures wandered around these woods at night, and a little shiver passed through him.

Then he heard a strange crackling sound...and an eerie glow
came shining through the trees that made his fur stand on end.

"It's Willard!" screamed Buford.
Colonel Katz came running towards him with his flashlight and crackling walkie-talkie. "Where have you been? The whole camp has been out searching for you!" He sounded both angry and happy at the same time.

"I ran away," said Willard.

"Why?" asked Colonel Katz.

"Because," said Willard, "the food is yucky and we fell in the lake and I sat on a doll house and there were no marshmallows at the campfire and I got poison ivy and our sleeping bags were glued shut and—worst of all—we had skunks in our bunks!"

"Yeah," grinned Buford, "it's been the best summer ever!" All the other kids laughed. And Willard had to admit that maybe Buford was right—maybe it had been fun in a crazy kind of way.

After a short lecture from Katz on the folly of running away from camp, everyone gathered around a campfire and toasted marshmallows (the new shipment had come in that afternoon) and sang loud, rowdy camp songs.

Later, Willard didn't even mind when Buford started acting goofy and wrote "WELCOME BACK, WILLARD!" on the bathroom mirror, then brushed his teeth with shampoo.

The next day during the big softball game against Camp Runamuck, Willard made a spectacular catch that saved the day.

As he was being carried off the field on the shoulders of his teammates, Willard realized it was his last day at Camp Catastrophe. A vacation that once seemed like it would never end was ending too soon.

Later everyone boarded the bus for the trip home. Willard took a seat by the window for one last look around—well, maybe not a last look. There was always next year.

ATASTROPHE